Mary Eleanor Wilkins Freeman

Evelina's Garden

Mary Eleanor Wilkins Freeman

Evelina's Garden

ISBN/EAN: 9783743383364

Manufactured in Europe, USA, Canada, Australia, Japa

Cover: Foto ©Andreas Hilbeck / pixelio.de

Manufactured and distributed by brebook publishing software
(www.brebook.com)

Mary Eleanor Wilkins Freeman

Evelina's Garden

EVELINA'S GARDEN

By Mary E. Wilkins

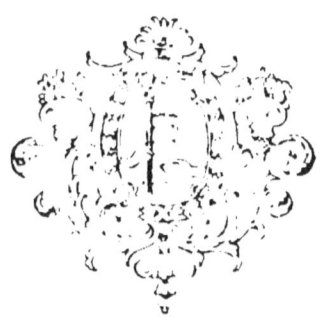

NEW YORK AND LONDON
HARPER & BROTHERS

MDCCCXCIX

EVELINA'S GARDEN

Evelina's Garden

On the south a high arbor-vitæ
hedge separated Evelina's garden
from the road. The hedge was so
high that when the school-children
lagged by, and the secrets behind it
fired them with more curiosity than
those between their battered book
covers, the tallest of them by stretch-
ing up on tiptoe could not peer over.
And so they were driven to childish
engineering feats, and would set to
work and pick away sprigs of the
arbor-vitæ with their little fingers,
and make peep-holes — but small
ones, that Evelina might not discern
them. Then they would thrust their
pink faces into the hedge, and the
enduring fragrance of it would come

3

to their nostrils like a gust of aromatic breath from the mouth of the northern woods, and peer into Evelina's garden as through the green tubes of vernal telescopes.

Then suddenly hollyhocks, blooming in rank and file, seemed to be marching upon them like platoons of soldiers, with detonations of color that dazzled their peeping eyes; and, indeed, the whole garden seemed charging with its mass of riotous bloom upon the hedge. They could scarcely take in details of marigold and phlox and pinks and London-pride and cock's-combs, and prince's-feathers waving overhead like standards.

Sometimes also there was the purple flutter of Evelina's gown; and Evelina's face, delicately faded, hung about with softly drooping gray curls, appeared suddenly among the flowers, like another flower uncannily instinct with nervous melancholy.

4

Then the children would fall back from their peep-holes, and huddle off together with scared giggles. They were afraid of Evelina. There was a shade of mystery about her which stimulated their childish fancies when they heard her discussed by their elders. They might easily have conceived her to be some baleful fairy intrenched in her green stronghold, withheld from leaving it by the fear of some dire penalty for magical sins. Summer and winter, spring and fall, Evelina Adams never was seen outside her own domain of old mansion-house and garden, and she had not set her slim lady feet in the public highway for nearly forty years, if the stories were true.

People differed as to the reason why. Some said she had had an unfortunate love affair, that her heart had been broken, and she had taken upon herself a vow of seclusion from the world, but nobody could

5

point to the unworthy lover who had done her this harm. When Evelina was a girl, not one of the young men of the village had dared address her. She had been set apart by birth and training, and also by a certain exclusiveness of manner, if not of nature. Her father, old Squire Adams, had been the one man of wealth and college learning in the village. He had owned the one fine old mansion-house, with its white front propped on great Corinthian pillars, overlooking the village like a broad brow of superiority.

He had owned the only coach and four. His wife during her short life had gone dressed in rich brocades and satins that rustled loud in the ears of the village women, and her nodding plumes had dazzled the eyes under their modest hoods. Hardly a woman in the village but could tell —for it had been handed down like a folk-lore song from mother to daughter—just what Squire Adams's wife wore when she walked out first as bride to meeting. She had been clad all in blue.

" Squire Adams's wife, when she walked out bride, she wore a blue satin brocade gown, all wrought with blue flowers of a darker blue, cut low neck and short sleeves. She wore long blue silk mitts wrought with blue, blue satin shoes, and blue silk clocked stockings. And she wore a blue crape mantle that was brought from over-seas, and a blue velvet hat, with a long blue ostrich feather curled over it—it was so long it reached her shoulder, and waved when she walked; and she carried a little blue crape fan with ivory sticks." So the women and girls told each other when the Squire's bride had been dead nearly seventy years.

The blue bride attire was said to be still in existence, packed away in a cedar chest, as the Squire had ordered after his wife's death. '' He stood over the woman that took care of his wife whilst she packed the things away, and he never shed a tear, but she used to hear him a-goin' up to the north chamber nights, when he could n't sleep, to look at 'em,'' the women told.

People had thought the Squire would marry again. They said Evelina, who was only four years old, needed a mother, and they selected one and another of the good village girls. But the Squire never married. He had a single woman, who dressed in black silk, and wore always a black wrought veil over the side of her bonnet, come to live with them, to take charge of Evelina. She was said to be a distant relative of the Squire's wife, and was much looked up to by the village people, although she never did more than interlace, as

it were, the fringes of her garments
with theirs. " She 's stuck up,"
they said, and felt, curiously enough,
a certain pride in the fact when they
met her in the street and she ducked
her long chin stiffly into the folds of
her black shawl by way of salutation.

When Evelina was fifteen years
old this single woman died, and the
village women went to her funeral,
and bent over her lying in a last
helpless dignity in her coffin, and
stared with awed freedom at her cold
face. After that Evelina was sent
away to school, and did not return,
except for a yearly vacation, for six
years to come. Then she returned,
and settled down in her old home to
live out her life, and end her days in
a perfect semblance of peace, if it
were not peace.

Evelina never had any young
school friend to visit her; she had
never, so far as any one knew, a
friend of her own age. She lived

alone with her father and three old
servants.   She went to meeting, and
drove with the Squire in his chaise.
The coach was never used after his
wife's death, except to carry Evelina
to and from school.   She and the
Squire also took long walks, but
they never exchanged aught but the
merest civilities of good-days and
nods with the neighbors whom they
met, unless indeed the Squire had
some matter of business to discuss.
Then Evelina stood aside and waited,
her fair face drooping gravely aloof.
She was very pretty, with a gentle
high-bred prettiness that impressed
the village folk, although they looked
at it somewhat askance.

Evelina's figure was tall, and had
a fine slenderness; her silken skirts
hung straight from the narrow silk
ribbon that girt her slim waist; there
was a languidly graceful bend in her
long white throat; her long delicate
hands hung inertly at her sides

among her skirt folds, and were never
seen to clasp anything; her softly
clustering fair curls hung over her
thin blooming cheeks, and her face
could scarce be seen, unless, as she
seldom did, she turned and looked
full upon one. Then her dark blue
eyes, with a little nervous frown between them, shone out radiantly;
her thin lips showed a warm red,
and her beauty startled one.

Everybody wondered why she did
not have a lover, why some fine
young man had not been smitten by
her while she had been away at
school. They did not know that
the school had been situated in
another little village, the counter-
part of the one in which she had
been born, wherein a fitting mate
for a bird of her feather could hardly
be found. The simple young men
of the country-side were at once
attracted and intimidated by her.
They cast fond sly glances across the

meeting-house at her lovely face, but they were confused before her when they jostled her in the door- way and the rose and lavender scent of her lady garments came in their faces. Not one of them dared ac- cost her, much less march boldly upon the great Corinthian-pillared house, raise the brass knocker, and declare himself a suitor for the Squire's daughter.

One young man there was, in- deed, who treasured in his heart an experience so subtle and so slight that he could scarcely believe in it himself. He never recounted it to mortal soul, but kept it as a secret sacred between himself and his own nature, but something to be scoffed at and set aside by others.

It had happened one Sabbath day in summer, when Evelina had not been many years home from school, as she sat in the meeting-house in her Sabbath array of rose-colored satin

gown, and white bonnet trimmed
with a long white feather and a
little wreath of feathery green, that
of a sudden she raised her head and
turned her face, and her blue eyes
met this young man's full upon hers,
with all his heart in them, and it was
for a second as if her own heart
leaped to the surface, and he saw it,
although afterwards he scarce be-
lieved it to be true.

Then a pallor crept over Evelina's
delicately brilliant face. She turned
it away, and her curls falling softly
from under the green wreath on her
bonnet brim hid it. The young
man's cheeks were a hot red, and his
heart beat loudly in his ears when he
met her in the doorway after the
sermon was done. His eager, timor-
ous eyes sought her face, but she
never looked his way. She laid her
slim hand in its cream-colored silk
mitt on the Squire's arm; her satin
gown rustled softly as she passed

before him, shrinking against the wall to give her room, and a faint fragrance which seemed like the very breath of the unknown delicacy and exclusiveness of life came to his bewildered senses.

Many a time he cast furtive glances across the meeting-house at Evelina, but she never looked his way again. If his timid boy-eyes could have seen her cheek behind its veil of curls, he might have discovered that the color came and went before his glances, although it was strange how she could have been conscious of them; but he never knew.

And he also never knew how, when he walked past the Squire's house of a Sunday evening, dressed in his best, with his shoulders thrust consciously back, and the windows in the westering sun looked full of blank gold to his furtive eyes, Evelina was always peeping at him from behind a shutter, and he never dared go in.

His intuitions were not like hers,
and so nothing happened that might
have, and he never fairly knew what
he knew. But that he never told,
even to his wife when he married;
for his hot young blood grew weary
and impatient with this vain court-
ship, and he turned to one of his
villagemates,' who met him fairly
half way, and married her within a
year.

On the Sunday when he and his
bride first appeared in the meeting-
house Evelina went up the aisle
behind her father in an array of
flowered brocade, stiff with threads
of silver, so wonderful that people
all turned their heads to stare at
her. She wore also a new bonnet
of rose-colored satin, and her curls
were caught back a little, and her
face showed as clear and beautiful
as an angel's.

The young bridegroom glanced at
her once across the meeting-house,

then he looked at his bride in her gay wedding finery with a faithful look.

When Evelina met them in the doorway, after meeting was done, she bowed with a sweet cold grace to the bride, who courtesied blushingly in return, with an awkward sweep of her foot in the bridal satin shoe. The bridegroom did not look at Evelina at all. He held his chin well down in his stock with solemn embarrassment, and passed out stiffly, his bride on his arm.

Evelina, shining in the sun like a silver lily, went up the street, her father stalking beside her with stately swings of his cane, and that was the last time she was ever seen at meeting. Nobody knew why.

When Evelina was a little over thirty her father died. There was not much active grief for him in the village; he had really figured therein more as a stately monument of his

own grandeur than anything else.
He had been a man of little force
of character, and that little had
seemed to degenerate since his wife
died. An inborn dignity of manner
might have served to disguise his
weakness with any others than these
shrewd New-Englanders, but they
read him rightly. " The Squire
wa'n't ever one to set the river
a-fire," they said. Then, moreover,
he left none of his property to the
village to build a new meeting-
house or a town-house. It all went
to Evelina.

People expected that Evelina
would surely show herself in her
mourning at meeting the Sunday
after the Squire died, but she did
not. Moreover, it began to be
gradually discovered that she never
went out in the village street nor
crossed the boundaries of her own
domains after her father's death.
She lived in the great house with

her three servants—a man and his wife, and the woman who had been with her mother when she died. Then it was that Evelina's garden began. There had always been a garden at the back of the Squire's house, but not like this, and only a low fence had separated it from the road. Now one morning in the autumn the people saw Evelina's man-servant, John Darby, setting out the arbor-vitæ hedge, and in the spring after that there were ploughing and seed-sowing extending over a full half-acre, which later blossomed out in glory.

Before the hedge grew so high Evelina could be seen at work in her garden. She was often stooping over the flower-beds in the early morning when the village was first astir, and she moved among them with her watering-pot in the twilight —a shadowy figure that might, from her grace and her constancy to the flowers, have been Flora herself.

As the years went on, the arbor-vitæ hedge got each season a new growth and waxed taller, until Evelina could no longer be seen above it. That was an annoyance to people, because the quiet mystery of her life kept their curiosity alive, until it was in a constant struggle, as it were, with the green luxuriance of the hedge.

" John Darby had ought to trim that hedge," they said. They accosted him in the street: " John, if ye don't cut that hedge down a little it 'll all die out." But he only made a surly grunting response, intelligible to himself alone, and passed on. He was an Englishman, and had lived in the Squire's family since he was a boy.

He had a nature capable of only one simple line of force, with no radiations or parallels, and that had early resolved itself into the service of the Squire and his house. After the Squire's death he married a woman who lived in the family. She was much older than himself, and had a high temper, but was a good servant, and he married her to keep her to her allegiance to Evelina. Then he bent her, without her knowledge, to take his own attitude towards his mistress. No more could be gotten out of John Darby's wife than out of John Darby concerning the doings at the Squire's house. She met curiosity with a flash of hot temper, and he with surly taciturnity, and both intimidated.

The third of Evelina's servants was the woman who had nursed her mother, and she was naturally subdued and undemonstrative, and rendered still more so by a ceaseless monotony of life. She never went to meeting, and was seldom seen outside the house. A passing vision of a long white-capped face at a window was about all the neighbors ever saw of this woman.

So Evelina's gentle privacy was well guarded by her own household, as by a faithful system of domestic police. She grew old peacefully behind her green hedge, shielded effectually from all rough bristles of curiosity. Every new spring her own bloom showed paler beside the new bloom of her flowers, but people could not see it.

Some thirty years after the Squire's death the man John Darby died; his wife, a year later. That left Evelina alone with the old woman who had nursed her mother. She was very old, but not feeble, and quite able to perform the simple household tasks for herself and Evelina. An old man, who saved himself from the almshouse in such ways, came daily to do the rougher part of the garden-work in John Darby's stead.

He was aged and decrepit; his muscles seemed able to perform their appointed tasks only through the accumulated inertia of a patiently toilsome life in the same tracks. Apparently they would have collapsed had he tried to force them to aught else than the holding of the ploughshare, the pulling of weeds, the digging around the roots of flowers, and the planting of seeds.

Every autumn he seemed about to totter to his fall among the fading flowers; every spring it was like Death himself urging on the resurrection; but he lived on year after year, and tended well Evelina's garden, and the gardens of other maidenwomen and widows in the village. He was taciturn, grubbing among his green beds as silently as a worm, but now and then he warmed a little under a fire of questions concerning Evelina's garden. " Never see none sech flowers in nobody's garden in this town, not sence I knowed 'nough to tell a pink from a piny," he would mumble. His speech was thick; his words were all uncouthly slurred; the expression of his whole life had come more through his old knotted hands of labor than through his tongue. But he would wipe his forehead with his shirt-sleeve and lean a second on his spade, and his face would change at the mention of the garden. Its wealth of bloom illumined his old mind, and the roses and honeysuckles and pinks seemed for a second to be reflected in his bleared old eyes.

There had never been in the village such a garden as this of Evelina Adams's. All the old blooms which had come over the seas with the early colonists, and started as it were their own colony of flora in the new country, flourished there. The naturalized pinks and phlox and hollyhocks and the rest, changed a little

in color and fragrance by the conditions of a new climate and soil, were
all in Evelina's garden, and no one
dreamed what they meant to Evelina; and she did not dream herself,
for her heart was always veiled to
her own eyes, like the face of a nun.
The roses and pinks, the poppies and
heart's-ease, were to this maiden-
woman, who had innocently and
helplessly outgrown her maiden
heart, in the place of all the loves
of life which she had missed. Her
affections had forced an outlet in
roses; they exhaled sweetness in
pinks, and twined and clung in
honeysuckle-vines. The daffodils,
when they came up in the spring,
comforted her like the smiles of children; when she saw the first rose, her
heart leaped as at the face of a lover.

She had lost the one way of human
affection, but her feet had found a
little single side-track of love, which
gave her still a zest in the journey of

life.   Even in the winter Evelina had
her flowers, for she kept those that
would bear transplanting in pots, and
all the sunny windows in her house
were gay with them.   She would
also not let a rose leaf fall and waste
in the garden soil, or a sprig of
lavender or thyme.   She gathered
them all, and stored them away in
chests and drawers and old china
bowls—the whole house seemed laid
away in rose leaves and lavender.
Evelina's clothes gave out at every
motion that fragrance of dead flowers which is like the fragrance of the
past, and has a sweetness like that
of sweet memories.   Even the cedar
chest where Evelina's mother's blue
bridal array was stored had its till
heaped with rose leaves and lavender.

When Evelina was nearly seventy
years old the old nurse who had
lived with her her whole life died.
People wondered then what she
would do.   '' She can't live all

alone in that great house," they
said. But she did live there alone
six months, until spring, and people
used to watch her evening lamp
when it was put out, and the morning smoke from her kitchen chimney.
" It ain't safe for her to be there
alone in that great house," they said.

But early in April a young girl
appeared one Sunday in the old
Squire's pew. Nobody had seen
her come to town, and nobody knew
who she was or where she came
from, but the old people said she
looked just as Evelina Adams used
to when she was young, and she
must be some relation. The old
man who had used to look across
the meeting-house at Evelina, over
forty years ago, looked across now
at this young girl, and gave a great
start, and his face paled under his
gray beard stubble. His old wife
gave an anxious, wondering glance
at him, and crammed a peppermint

into his hand. "Anything the matter, father?" she whispered; but he
only gave his head a half-surly shake,
and then fastened his eyes straight
ahead upon the pulpit. He had
reason to that day, for his only son,
Thomas, was going to preach his
first sermon therein as a candidate.
His wife ascribed his nervousness to
that. She put a peppermint in her
own mouth and sucked it comfort-
ably. " That 's all 't is," she
thought to herself. " Father always
was easy worked up," and she
looked proudly up at her son sitting
on the hair-cloth sofa in the pulpit,
leaning his handsome young head
on his hand, as he had seen old
divines do. She never dreamed that
her old husband sitting beside her
was possessed of an inner life so
strange to her that she would not
have known him had she met him
in the spirit. And, indeed, it had
been so always, and she had never

dreamed of it. Although he had been faithful to his wife, the image of Evelina Adams in her youth, and that one love-look which she had given him, had never left his soul, but had given it a guise and complexion of which his nearest and dearest knew nothing.

It was strange; but now, as he looked up at his own son as he arose in the pulpit, he could seem to see a look of that fair young Evelina, who had never had a son to inherit her beauty. He had certainly a delicate brilliancy of complexion, which he could have gotten directly from neither father nor mother; and whence came that little nervous frown between his dark blue eyes? His mother had blue eyes, but not like his; they flashed over the great pulpit Bible with a sweet fire that matched the memory in his father's heart.

But the old man put the fancy

away from him in a minute; it was one which his stern common-sense always overcame. It was impossible that Thomas Merriam should resemble Evelina Adams; indeed, people always called him the very image of his father.

The father tried to fix his mind upon his son's sermon, but presently he glanced involuntarily across the meeting-house at the young girl, and again his heart leaped and his face paled; but he turned his eyes gravely back to the pulpit, and his wife did not notice. Now and then she thrust a sharp elbow in his side to call his attention to a grand point in their son's discourse. The odor of peppermint was strong in his nostrils, but through it all he seemed to perceive the rose and lavender scent of Evelina Adams's youthful garments. Whether it was with him simply the memory of an odor, which affected him like the odor itself, or not, those

in the vicinity of the Squire's pew
were plainly aware of it. The gown
which the strange young girl wore
was, as many an old woman discovered to her neighbor with loud
whispers, one of Evelina's, which
had been laid away in a sweet-smell-
ing chest since her old girlhood. It
had been somewhat altered to suit
the fashion of a later day, but the
eyes which had fastened keenly upon
it when Evelina first wore it up the
meeting-house aisle could not mis-
take it. "It's Evelina Adams's
lavender satin made over," one whispered, with a sharp hiss of breath,
in the other's ear.

The lavender satin, deepening into
purple in the folds, swept in a rich
circle over the knees of the young
girl in the Squire's pew. She folded
her little hands, which were encased
in Evelina's cream-colored silk mitts,
over it, and looked up at the young
minister, and listened to his sermon

with a grave and innocent dignity,
as Evelina had done before her.
Perhaps the resemblance between
this young girl and the young girl of
the past was more one of mien than
aught else, although the type of face
was the same. This girl had the
same fine sharpness of feature and
delicately bright color, and she also
wore her hair in curls, although they
were tied back from her face with a
black velvet ribbon, and did not veil
it when she drooped her head, as
Evelina's used to do.

The people divided their attention
between her and the new minister.
Their curiosity goaded them in equal
measure with their spiritual zeal.
" I can't wait to find out who that
girl is," one woman whispered to
another.

The girl herself had no thought of
the commotion which she awakened.
When the service was over, and
she walked with a gentle maiden

stateliness, which seemed a very
copy of Evelina's own, out of the
meeting-house, down the street to the
Squire's house, and entered it, passing under the stately Corinthian pillars, with a last purple gleam of her
satin skirts, she never dreamed of
the eager attention that followed
her.

It was several days before the
village people discovered who she
was. The information had to be
obtained, by a process like mental
thumb-screwing, from the old man
who tended Evelina's garden, but at
last they knew. She was the daughter of a cousin of Evelina's on the
father's side. Her name was Evelina Leonard; she had been named
for her father's cousin. She had
been finely brought up, and had attended a Boston school for young
ladies. Her mother had been dead
many years, and her father had died
some two years ago, leaving her with

only a very little money, which was now all gone, and Evelina Adams had invited her to live with her. Evelina Adams had herself told the old gardener, seeing his scant curiosity was somewhat awakened by the sight of the strange young lady in the garden, but he seemed to have almost forgotten it when the people questioned him.

" She 'll leave her all her money, most likely," they said, and they looked at this new Evelina in the old Evelina's perfumed gowns with awe.

However, in the space of a few months the opinion upon this matter was divided. Another cousin of Evelina Adams's came to town, and this time an own cousin—a widow in fine black bombazine, portly and florid, walking with a majestic swell, and, moreover, having with her two daughters, girls of her own type, not so far advanced. This woman

c

hired one of the village cottages, and it was rumored that Evelina Adams paid the rent. Still, it was considered that she was not very intimate with these last relatives. The neighbors watched, and saw, many a time, Mrs. Martha Loomis and her girls try the doors of the Adams house, scudding around angrily from front to side and back, and knock and knock again, but with no admittance. " Evelina she won't let none of 'em in more 'n once a week," the neighbors said. It was odd that, although they had deeply resented Evelina's seclusion on their own accounts, they were rather on her side in this matter, and felt a certain delight when they witnessed a crestfallen retreat of the widow and her daughters. " I don't s'pose she wants them Loomises marchin' in on her every minute," they said.

The new Evelina was not seen

much with the other cousins, and
she made no acquaintances in the
village. Whether she was to inherit
all the Adams property or not, she
seemed, at any rate, heiress to all
the elder Evelina's habits of life.
She worked with her in the garden,
and wore her old girlish gowns, and
kept almost as close at home as she.
She often, however, walked abroad
in the early dusk, stepping along in
a grave and stately fashion, as the
elder Evelina had used to do, holding her skirts away from the dewy
roadside weeds, her face showing
out in the twilight like a white
flower, as if it had a pale light of its
own.

Nobody spoke to her ; people
turned furtively after she had passed
and stared after her, but they never
spoke. This young Evelina did not
seem to expect it. She passed along
with the lids cast down over her blue
eyes, and the rose and lavender scent

of her garments came back in their
faces.

But one night when she was walking slowly along, a full half-mile
from home, she heard rapid foot-
steps behind, and the young minister, Thomas Merriam, came up
beside her and spoke.

" Good-evening," said he, and
his voice was a little hoarse through
nervousness.

Evelina started, and turned her
fair face up towards his. " Good-
evening," she responded, and courtesied as she had been taught at school,
and stood close to the wall, that he
might pass; but Thomas Merriam
paused also.

" I— " he began, but his voice
broke. He cleared his throat angrily, and went on. " I have seen
you in meeting," he said, with a
kind of defiance, more of himself
than of her. After all, was he not
the minister, and had he not the

right to speak to everybody in the
congregation ? Why should he em-
barrass himself ?

" Yes, sir," replied Evelina. She
stood drooping her head before him,
and yet there was a certain delicate
hauteur about her. Thomas was
afraid to speak again. They both
stood silent for a moment, and then
Evelina stirred softly, as if to pass
on, and Thomas spoke out bravely.
" Is your cousin, Miss Adams,
well ?" said he.

" She is pretty well, I thank you,
sir."

" I have been wanting to—call,"
he began; then he hesitated again.
His handsome young face was blush-
ing crimson.

Evelina's own color deepened.
She turned her face away. " Cousin
Evelina never sees callers," she said,
with grave courtesy; " perhaps you
did not know. She has not for a
great many years."

" Yes, I did know it," returned
Thomas Merriam ; "that 's the
reason I have n't called."

" Cousin Evelina is not strong,"
remarked the young girl, and there
was a savor of apology in her
tone.

" But — " stammered Thomas;
then he stopped again. " May I—
has she any objections to—anybody's coming to see you ? "

Evelina started. " I am afraid
Cousin Evelina would not approve,"
she answered, primly. Then she
looked up in his face, and a girlish
piteousness came into her own. " I
am very sorry," she said, and there
was a catch in her voice.

Thomas bent over her impetu-
ously. All his ministerial state fell
from him like an outer garment of
the soul. He was young, and he
had seen this girl Sunday after Sunday. He had written all his sermons
with her image before his eyes,

38

he had preached to her, and her
only, and she had come between his
heart and all the nations of the earth
in his prayers. " Oh," he stammered out, " I am afraid you can't
be very happy living there the way
you do. Tell me— "

Evelina turned her face away with
sudden haughtiness. " My cousin
Evelina is very kind to me, sir," she
said.

" But — you must be lonesome
with nobody—of your own age—to
speak to," persisted Thomas, con-
fusedly.

" I never cared much for youthful
company. It is getting dark; I
must be going," said Evelina. " I
wish you good-evening, sir."

" Sha'n't I — walk home with
you ?" asked Thomas, falteringly.

" It is n't necessary, thank you,
and I don't think Cousin Evelina
would approve," she replied, primly ;
and her light dress fluttered away

into the dusk and out of sight like
the pale wing of a moth.

Poor Thomas Merriam walked on
with his head in a turmoil. His
heart beat loud in his ears. " I 've
made her mad with me," he said to
himself, using the old rustic school-
boy vernacular, from which he did
not always depart in his thoughts,
although his ministerial dignity
guarded his conversations. Thomas
Merriam came of a simple homely
stock, whose speech came from the
emotions of the heart, all unregu-
lated by the usages of the schools.
He was the first for generations who
had aspired to college learning and
a profession, and had trained his
tongue by the models of the edu-
cated and polite. He could not
help, at times, the relapse of his
thoughts, and their speaking to himself in the dialect of his family and
his ancestors. " She 's 'way above
me, and I ought to ha' known it,"

he further said, with the meekness
of an humble but fiercely independ-
ent race, which is meek to itself
alone. He would have maintained
his equality with his last breath to
an opponent; in his heart of hearts
he felt himself below the scion of the
one old gentle family of his native
village.

This young Evelina, by the fine
dignity which had been born with
her and not acquired by precept and
example, by the sweetly formal
diction which seemed her native
tongue, had filled him with awe.
Now, when he thought she was angered with him, he felt beneath her
lady feet, his nostrils choked with a
spiritual dust of humiliation.

He went forward blindly. The
dusk had deepened; from either side
of the road, from the mysterious
gloom of the bushes, came the twangs
of the katydids, like some coarse
rustic quarrellers, each striving for

the last word in a dispute not even dignified by excess of passion.

Suddenly somebody jostled him to his own side of the path. "That you, Thomas? Where you been?" said a voice in his ear.

"That you, father? Down to the post-office."

"Who was that you was talkin' with back there?"

"Miss Evelina Leonard."

"That girl that 's stayin' there—to the old Squire's?"

"Yes." The son tried to move on, but his father stood before him dumbly for a minute. "I must be going, father. I 've got to work on my sermon," Thomas said, impatiently.

"Wait a minute," said his father. "I 've got something to say to ye, Thomas, an' this is as good a time to say it as any. There ain't anybody 'round. I don't know as ye 'll thank me for it—but mother said

the other day that she thought
you 'd kind of an idea—she said you
asked her if she thought it would be
anything out of the way for you to
go up to the Squire's to make a
call.   Mother she thinks you can
step in anywheres, but I don't know.
I know your book-learnin' and your
bein' a minister has set you up a
good deal higher than your mother
and me and any of our folks, and I
feel as if you were good enough for
anybody, as far as that goes; but
that ain't all.   Some folks have different startin'-points in this world,
and they see things different; and
when they do, it ain't much use
tryin' to make them walk alongside
and see things alike.   Their eyes have
got different cants, and they ain't
able to help it.   Now this girl she 's
related to the old Squire, and
she 's been brought up different, and
she started ahead, even if her father
did lose all his property.   She 'ain't

never eat in the kitchen, nor been
scart to set down in the parlor, and
satin and velvet, and silver spoons,
and cream-pots 'ain't never looked
anything out of the common to her,
and they always will to you. No
matter how many such things you
may live to have, they 'll always get
a little the better of ye. She 'll be
'way above 'em; and you won't, no
matter how hard you try. Some
ideas can't never mix; and when
ideas can't mix, folks can't.''

"I never said they could," returned Thomas, shortly. " I can't
stop to talk any longer, father. I
must go home."

" No, you wait a minute, Thomas.
I 'm goin' to say out what I started
to, and then I sha'n't ever bring it
up again. What I was comin' at
was this: I wanted to warn ye a
little. You must n't set too much
store by little things that you think
mean consider'ble when they don't.

44

Looks don't count for much, and I
want you to remember it, and not be
upset by 'em.''

Thomas gave a great start and
colored high. '' I 'd like to know
what you mean, father,'' he cried,
sharply.

'' Nothin'. I don't mean nothin',
only I 'm older 'n you, and it 's
come in my way to know some
things, and it 's fittin' you should
profit by it. A young woman's looks
at you don't count for much. I
don't s'pose she knows why she
gives 'em herself half the time; they
ain't like us. It 's best you should
make up your mind to it; if you
don't, you may find it out by the
hardest. That 's all. I ain't never
goin' to bring this up again.''

'' I 'd like to know what you
mean, father.'' Thomas's voice
shook with embarrassment and
anger.

'' I ain't goin' to say anything

45

more about it," replied the old man. " Mary Ann Pease and Arabella Mann are both in the settin'-room with your mother. I thought I 'd tell ye, in case ye did n't want to see 'em, and wanted to go to work on your sermon."

Thomas made an impatient ejaculation as he strode off. When he reached the large white house where he lived he skirted it carefully. The chirping treble of girlish voices came from the open sitting-room window, and he caught a glimpse of a smooth brown head and a high shell comb in front of the candle-light. The young minister tiptoed in the back door and across the kitchen to the back stairs. The sitting-room door was open, and the candle-light streamed out, and the treble voices rose high. Thomas, advancing through the dusky kitchen with cautious steps, encountered suddenly a chair in the dark corner by the stairs, and just saved himself from falling. There was a startled outcry from the sitting-room, and his mother came running into the kitchen with a candle.

"Who is it?" she demanded, valiantly. Then she started and gasped as her son confronted her. He shook a furious warning fist at the sitting-room door and his mother, and edged towards the stairs. She followed him close. "Had n't you better jest step in a minute?" she whispered. "Them girls have been here an hour, and I know they 're waitin' to see you." Thomas shook his head fiercely, and swung himself around the corner into the dark crook of the back stairs. His mother thrust the candle into his hand. "Take this, or you 'll break your neck on them stairs," she whispered.

Thomas, stealing up the stairs like a cat, heard one of the girls call to his mother—"Is it robbers, Mis'

Merriam ? Want us to come an'
help tackle 'em ?''—and he fairly
shuddered; for Evelina's gentle-lady
speech was still in his ears, and this
rude girlish call seemed to jar upon
his sensibilities.

" The idea of any girl screeching
out like that,'' he muttered. And
if he had carried speech as far as his
thought, he would have added,
" when Evelina is a girl! ''

He was so angry that he did not
laugh when he heard his mother answer back, in those conclusive tones
of hers that were wont to silence all
argument : " It ain't anything.
Don't be scared. I 'm coming right
back.'' Mrs. Merriam scorned sub-
terfuges. She took always a silent
stand in a difficulty, and let people
infer what they would. When Mary
Ann Pease inquired if it was the cat
that had made the noise, she asked
if her mother had finished her blue
and white counterpane.

The two girls waited a half-hour longer, then they went home. "What do you s'pose made that noise out in the kitchen?" asked Arabella Mann of Mary Ann Pease, the minute they were out-of-doors.

"I don't know," replied Mary Ann Pease. She was a broad-backed young girl, and looked like a matron as she hurried along in the dusk.

"Well, I know what I think it was," said Arabella Mann, moving ahead with sharp jerks of her little dark body.

"What?"

"It was him."

"You don't mean—"

"I think it was Thomas Merriam, and he was tryin' to get up the back stairs unbeknownst to anybody, and he run into something."

"What for?"

"Because he did n't want to see *us*."

"Now, Arabella Mann, I don't

believe it! He's always real pleas-
ant to me."

"Well, I do believe it, and I
guess he'll know it when I set foot
in that house again. I guess he'll
find out I did n't go there to see
him! He need n't feel so fine, if he
is the minister; his folks ain't any
better than mine, an' we've got
'nough sight handsomer furniture in
our parlor."

"Did you see how the tallow had
all run down over the candles?"

"Yes, I did. She gave that candle
she carried out in the kitchen to him,
too. Mother says she was n't never
any kind of a housekeeper."

"Hush! Arabella: here he is
coming now."

But it was not Thomas; it was his
father, advancing through the evening with his son's gait and carriage.
When the two girls discovered that,
one tittered out quite audibly, and
they scuttled past. They were not

rivals; they simply walked faithfully
side by side in pursuit of the young
minister, giving him as it were an
impartial choice.   There were even
no heart-burnings between them;
one always confided in the other
when she supposed herself to have
found some slight favor in Thomas's
sight; and, indeed, the young minister could scarcely bow to one upon
the street unless she flew to the other
with the news.

Thomas Merriam himself was
aware of all this devotion on the
part of the young women of his
flock, and it filled him with a sort
of angry shame.   He could not
have told why, but he despised
himself for being the object of their
attention more than he despised
them.   His heart sank at the idea
of Evelina's discovering it.   What
would she think of him if she knew
all those young women haunted his
house and lagged after meeting on

the chance of getting a word from him ? Suppose she should see their eyes upon his face in meeting time, and decipher their half-unconscious boldness, as he had done against his will. Once Evelina had looked at him, even as the older Evelina had looked at his father, and all other looks of maidens seemed to him like profanations of that, even although he doubted afterwards that he had rightly interpreted it. Full it had seemed to him of that tender maiden surprise and wonder, of that love that knows not itself, and sees its own splendor for the first time in another's face, and flees at the sight. It had happened once when he was coming down the aisle after the sermon and Evelina had met him at the door of her pew. But she had turned her head quickly, and her soft curls flowed over her red cheek, and he doubted ever after if he had read the look aright. When he had

gotten the courage to speak to her,
and she had met him with the gentle
coldness which she had learned of
her lady aunt and her teacher in
Boston, his doubt was strong upon
him. The next Sunday he looked
not her way at all. He even tried
faithfully from day to day to drive
her image from his mind with prayer
and religious thoughts, but in spite
of himself he would lapse into dreams
about her, as if borne by a current of
nature too strong to be resisted.
And sometimes, upon being awakened from them, as he sat over his
sermon with the ink drying on his
quill, by the sudden outburst of
treble voices in his mother's sitting-
room below, the fancy would seize
him that possibly these other young
damsels took fond liberties with him
in their dreams, as he with Evelina,
and he resented it with a fierce
maidenliness of spirit, although he
was a man. The thought that

possibly they, over their spinning or
their quilting, had in their hearts the
image of himself with fond words
upon his lips and fond looks in his
eyes, filled him with shame and rage,
although he took the same liberty
with the delicately haughty maiden
Evelina.

But Thomas Merriam was not
given to undue appreciation of his
own fascination, as was proved by
his ready discouragement in the case
of Evelina. He had the knowledge
of his conquests forced upon his
understanding until he could no
longer evade it. Every day were
offerings laid upon his shrine, of
pound-cakes and flaky pies, and
loaves of white bread, and cups of
jelly, whereby the culinary skill of
his devotees might be proved.
Silken purses and beautiful socks
knitted with fancy stitches, and holy
book-marks for his Bible, and even
a wonderful bedquilt, and a fine

linen shirt with hem-stitched bands,
poured in upon him. He burned
with angry blushes when his mother,
smiling meaningly, passed them over
to him. " Put them away, mother;
I don't want them," he would growl
out, in a distress that was half comic
and half pathetic. He would never
taste of the tempting viands which
were brought to him. " How you
act, Thomas!" his mother would
say. She was secretly elated by
these feminine libations upon the
altar of her son. They did not grate
upon her sensibilities, which were
not delicate. She even tried to
assist two or three of the young
women in their designs; she would
often praise them and their handi-
work to her son—and in this she was
aided by an old woman aunt of hers
who lived with the family. " Nancy
Winslow is as handsome a girl as
ever I set eyes on, an' I never see
any nicer sewin'," Mrs. Merriam

said, after the advent of the linen shirt, and she held it up to the light admiringly. "Jest look at that hem-stitchin'!" she said.

"I guess whoever made that shirt calkilated 't would do for a weddin' one," said old Aunt Betty Green, and Thomas made an exclamation and went out of the room, tingling all over with shame and disgust.

"Thomas don't act nateral," said the old woman, glancing after him through her iron-bound spectacles.

"I dun'no' what 's got into him," returned his mother.

"Mebbe they foller him up a leetle too close," said Aunt Betty. "I dun'no' as I should have ventured on a shirt when I was a gal. I made a satin vest once for Joshua, but that don't seem quite as p'inted as a shirt. It did n't scare Joshua, nohow. He asked me to have him the next week."

" Well, I dun'no'," said Mrs. Merriam again. " I kind of wish Thomas would settle on somebody, for I 'm pestered most to death with 'em, an' I feel as if 't was kind of mean takin' all these things into the house."

" They 've 'bout kept ye in sweet cake, 'ain't they, lately?"

" Yes; but I don't feel as if it was jest right for us to eat it up, when 't was brought for Thomas. But he won't touch it. I can't see as he has the least idee of any one of them. I don't believe Thomas has ever seen anybody he wanted for a wife."

" Well, he 's got the pick of 'em, a-settin' their caps right in his face," said Aunt Betty.

Neither of them dreamed how the young man, sleeping and eating and living under the same roof, beloved of them since he entered the world, holding himself coldly aloof from this crowd of half-innocently, half-boldly ardent young women, had set up for himself his own divinity of love, before whom he consumed himself in vain worship. His father suspected, and that was all, and he never mentioned the matter again to his son.

After Thomas had spoken to Evelina the weeks went on, and they never exchanged another word, and their eyes never met. But they dwelt constantly within each other's thoughts, and were ever present to each other's spiritual vision. Always as the young minister bent over his sermon-paper, laboriously tracing out with sputtering quill his application of the articles of the orthodox faith, Evelina's blue eyes seemed to look out at him between the stern doctrines like the eyes of an angel. And he could not turn the pages of the Holy Writ unless he found some passage therein which to his mind treated directly of her, setting forth her graces like a prophecy. " The fairest among women," read Thomas Merriam, and nodded his head, while his heart leaped with the satisfied delight of all its fancies, at the image of his love's fair and gentle face. " Her price is far above rubies," read Thomas Merriam, and he nodded his head again, and saw Evelina shining as with gold and pearls, more precious than all the jewels of the earth. In spite of all his efforts, when Thomas Merriam studied the Scriptures in those days he was more nearly touched by those old human hearts which throbbed down to his through the ages, welding the memories of their old loves to his living one until they seemed to prove its eternity, than by the Messianic prophecies. Often he spent hours upon his knees, but arose with Evelina's face before his very soul in spite of all.

And as for Evelina, she tended the flowers in the elder Evelina's garden with her poor cousin, whose own love-dreams had been illustrated as it were by the pinks and lilies blooming around them when they had all gone out of her heart, and Thomas Merriam's half-bold, half-imploring eyes looked up at her out of every flower and stung her heart like bees. Poor young Evelina feared much lest she had offended Thomas, and yet her own maiden decorum had been offended by him, and she had offended it herself, and she was faint with shame and distress when she thought of it. How had she been so bold and shameless as to give him that look at the meeting-house ? and how had he been so cruel as to accost her afterwards ? She told herself she had done right for the maintenance of her own maiden dignity, and yet she feared lest she had angered him and hurt him.

" Suppose he had been fretted by
her coolness ?" she thought, and
then a great wave of tender pity
went over her heart, and she would
almost have spoken to him of her
own accord. But then she would
reflect how he continued to write
such beautiful sermons, and prove
so clearly and logically the tenets of
the faith; and how could he do that
with a mind in distress ? Scarcely
could she herself tend the flower-
beds as she should, nor set her embroidery stitches finely and evenly,
she was so ill at ease. It must be
that Thomas had not given the matter an hour's worry, since he continued to do his work so faithfully
and well. And then her own heart
would be sorer than ever with the
belief that his was happy and at
rest, although she would chide herself for it.

And yet this young Evelina was a
philosopher and an analyst of human

nature in a small way, and she got
some slight comfort out of a shrewd
suspicion that the heart of a man
might love and suffer on a somewhat
different principle from the heart of
a woman. " It may be," thought
Evelina, sitting idle over her embroidery with far-away blue eyes,
" that a man's heart can always turn
a while from love to other things as
weighty and serious, although he be
just as fond, while a woman's heart
is always fixed one way by loving,
and cannot be turned unless it breaks.
And it may be wise," thought young
Evelina, " else how could the state
be maintained and governed, battles
for independence be fought, and
even souls be saved, and the gospel
carried to the heathen, if men could
not turn from the concerns of their
own hearts more easily than women ?
Women should be patient," thought
Evelina, " and consider that if they
suffer 't is due to the lot which a

wise Providence has given them."
And yet tears welled up in her earnest blue eyes and fell over her fair
cheeks and wet the embroidery—
when the elder Evelina was not looking, as she seldom was. The elder
Evelina was kind to her young
cousin, but there were days when
she seemed to dwell alone in her
own thoughts, apart from the
whole world, and she seldom spoke
either to Evelina or her old servant-
man.

Young Evelina, trying to atone
for her former indiscretion and es-
tablish herself again on her height of
maiden reserve in Thomas Merriam's
eyes, sat resolutely in the meeting-
house of a Sabbath day, with her
eyes cast down, and after service she
glided swiftly down the aisle and
was out of the door before the young
minister could much more than de-
scend the pulpit stairs, unless he ran
an indecorous race.

And young Evelina never at twilight strolled up the road in the direction of Thomas Merriam's home, where she might quite reasonably hope to meet him, since he was wont to go to the store when the evening stage-coach came in with the mail from Boston.

Instead she paced the garden paths, or, when there was not too heavy a dew, rambled across the fields; and there was also a lane where she loved to walk. Whether or not Thomas Merriam suspected this, or had ever seen, as he passed the mouth of the lane, the flutter of maidenly draperies in the distance, it so happened that one evening he also went a-walking there, and met Evelina. He had entered the lane from the highway, and she from the fields at the head. So he saw her first afar off, and could not tell fairly whether her light muslin skirt might not be only a white-flowering bush.

64

For, since his outlook upon life had
been so full of Evelina, he had found
that often the most common and
familiar things would wear for a
second a look of her to startle him.
And many a time his heart had
leaped at the sight of a white bush
ahead stirring softly in the evening
wind, and he had thought it might
be she.   Now he said to himself impatiently that this was only another
fancy; but soon he saw that it was
indeed Evelina, in a light muslin
gown, with a little lace kerchief on
her head.   His handsome young face
was white; his lips twitched nerv-
ously; but he reached out and pulled
a spray of white flowers from a bush,
and swung it airily to hide his agita-
tion as he advanced.

As for Evelina, when she first
espied Thomas she started and half
turned, as if to go back; then she
held up her white-kerchiefed head
with gentle pride and kept on. When

she came up to Thomas she walked
so far to one side that her muslin
skirt was in danger of catching and
tearing on the bushes, and she never
raised her eyes, and not a flicker of
recognition stirred her sweet pale
face as she passed him.

But Thomas started as if she had
struck him, and dropped his spray
of white flowers, and could not help
a smothered cry that was half a sob,
as he went on, knocking blindly
against the bushes. He went a little
way, then he stopped and looked
back with his piteous hurt eyes.
And Evelina had stopped also, and
she had the spray of white flowers
which he had dropped, in her hand,
and her eyes met his. Then she let
the flowers fall again, and clapped
both her little hands to her face to
cover it, and turned to run; but
Thomas was at her side, and he put
out his hand and held her softly by
her white arm.

66

"Oh," he panted, "I—did not mean to be—too presuming, and offend you. I—crave your pardon—"

Evelina had recovered herself. She stood with her little hands clasped, and her eyes cast down before him; but not a quiver stirred her pale face, which seemed turned to marble by this last effort of her maiden pride. "I have nothing to pardon," said she. "It was I, whose bold behavior, unbecoming a modest and well-trained young woman, gave rise to what seemed like presumption on your part." The sense of justice was strong within her, but she made her speech haughtily and primly, as if she had learned it by rote from some maiden school-mistress, and pulled her arm away and turned to go; but Thomas's words stopped her.

"Not—unbecoming if it came— from the heart," said he, brokenly, scarcely daring to speak, and yet not daring to be silent.

Then Evelina turned on him, with a sudden strange pride that lay beneath all other pride, and was of a nobler and truer sort. " Do you think I would have given you the look that I did if it had not come from my heart ? " she demanded. " What did you take me to be—false and a jilt ? I may be a forward young woman, who has overstepped the bounds of maidenly decorum, and I shall never get over the shame of it, but I am truthful, and I am no jilt." The brilliant color flamed out on Evelina's cheeks. Her blue eyes met Thomas's with that courage of innocence and nature which dares all shame. But it was only for a second; the tears sprang into them. " I beg you to let me go home," she said, pitifully; but Thomas caught her in his arms, and pressed her troubled maiden face against his breast.

" Oh, I love you so!" he whispered—" I love you so, Evelina,
and I was afraid you were angry
with me for it."

" And I was afraid," she faltered,
half weeping and half shrinking from
him, " lest you were angry with me
for betraying the state of my feel-
ings, when you could not return
them." And even then she used
that gentle formality of expression
with which she had been taught by
her maiden preceptors to veil de-
corously her most ardent emotions.
And, in truth, her training stood her
in good stead in other ways; for she
presently commanded, with that
mild dignity of hers which allowed
of no remonstrance, that Thomas
should take away his arm from her
waist, and give her no more kisses for
that time.

" It is not becoming for any one,"
said she, " and much less for a minister of the gospel. And as for

myself, I know not what Mistress
Perkins would say to me. She has
a mind much above me, I fear."

." Mistress Perkins is enjoying her
mind in Boston," said Thomas Merriam, with the laugh of a triumphant
young lover.

But Evelina did not laugh. "It
might be well for both you and me
if she were here," said she, seriously.
However, she tempered a little her
decorous following of Mistress Perkins's precepts, and she and Thomas
went hand in hand up the lane and
across the fields.

There was no dew that night, and
the moon was full. It was after
nine o'clock when Thomas left her
at the gate in the fence which separated Evelina Adams's garden from
the field, and watched her disappear
between the flowers. The moon
shone full on the garden. Evelina
walked as it were over a silver dapple,
which her light gown seemed to

brush away and dispel for a moment. The bushes stood in sweet
mysterious clumps of shadow.

Evelina had almost reached the
house, and was close to the great
althea bush, which cast a wide circle
of shadow, when it seemed suddenly
to separate and move into life.

The elder Evelina stepped out
from the shadow of the bush. " Is
that you, Evelina ? " she said, in her
soft, melancholy voice, which had in
it a nervous vibration.

" Yes, Cousin Evelina."

The elder Evelina's pale face,
drooped about with gray curls, had
an unfamiliar, almost uncanny, look
in the moonlight, and might have
been the sorrowful visage of some
marble nymph, lovelorn, with un-
ceasing grace. " Who—was with
you ? " she asked.

" The minister," replied young
Evelina.

" Did he meet you ? "

" He met me in the lane, Cousin Evelina."

" And he walked home with you across the field ? "

" Yes, Cousin Evelina."

Then the two entered the house, and nothing more was said about the matter. Young Evelina and Thomas Merriam agreed that their affection was to be kept a secret for a while. " For," said young Evelina, " I cannot leave Cousin Evelina yet a while, and I cannot have her pestered with thinking about it, at least before another spring, when she has the garden fairly growing again."

" That is nearly a whole year; it is August now," said Thomas, half reproachfully, and he tightened his clasp of Evelina's slender fingers.

" I cannot help that," replied Evelina. " It is for you to show Christian patience more than I, Thomas. If you could have seen poor Cousin Evelina, as I have seen

72

her, through the long winter days,
when her garden is dead, and she
has only the few plants in her window left! When she is not watering
and tending them she sits all day in
the window and looks out over the
garden and the naked bushes and
the withered flower-stalks. She used
not to be so, but would read her
Bible and good books, and busy herself somewhat over fine needle-work,
and at one time she was compiling a
little floral book, giving a list of the
flowers, and poetical selections and
sentiments appropriate to each.
That was her pastime for three win-
ters, and it is now nearly done; but
she has given that up, and all the
rest, and sits there in the window
and grows older and feebler until
spring. It is only I who can divert
her mind, by reading aloud to her
and singing; and sometimes I paint
the flowers she loves the best on
card-board with water-colors. I have

a poor skill in it, but Cousin Evelina can tell which flower I have tried to represent, and it pleases her greatly. I have even seen her smile. No, I cannot leave her, nor even pester her with telling her before another spring, and you must wait, Thomas," said young Evelina.

And Thomas agreed, as he was likely to do to all which she proposed which touched not his own sense of right and honor. Young Evelina gave Thomas one more kiss for his earnest pleading, and that night wrote out the tale in her journal. " It may be that I overstepped the bounds of maidenly decorum," wrote Evelina, " but my heart did so entreat me," and no blame whatever did she lay upon Thomas.

Young Evelina opened her heart only to her journal, and her cousin was told nothing, and had little cause for suspicion. Thomas Merriam never came to the house to see his sweetheart; he never walked home with her from meeting. Both were anxious to avoid village gossip, until the elder Evelina could be told.

Often in the summer evenings the lovers met, and strolled hand in hand across the fields, and parted at the garden gate with the one kiss which Evelina allowed, and that was all.

Sometimes when young Evelina came in with her lover's kiss still warm upon her lips the elder Evelina looked at her wistfully, with a strange retrospective expression in her blue eyes, as if she were striving to remember something that the girl's face called to mind. And yet she could have had nothing to remember except dreams.

And once, when young Evelina sat sewing through a long summer afternoon and thinking about her lover, the elder Evelina, who was storing rose leaves mixed with sweet spices in a jar, said, suddenly, " He looks as his father used to."

Young Evelina started. " Whom do you mean, Cousin Evelina ? " she asked, wonderingly; for the elder Evelina had not glanced at her, nor even seemed to address her at all.

" Nothing," said the elder Evelina, and a soft flush stole over her withered face and neck, and she sprinkled more cassia on the rose leaves in the jar.

Young Evelina said no more; but she wondered, partly because Thomas was always in her mind, and it seemed to her naturally that nearly everything must have a savor of meaning of him, if her cousin Evelina could possibly have referred to him and his likeness to his father. For it was commonly said that Thomas looked very like his father, although his figure was different. The young man was taller and more firmly built, and he had not the meek forward curve of shoulder which had grown upon his father of late years.

When the frosty nights came Thomas and Evelina could not meet and walk hand in hand over the fields behind the Squire's house, and they very seldom could speak to each other. It was nothing except a " good-day " on the street, and a stolen glance, which set them both a-trembling lest all the congregation had noticed, in the meeting-house. When the winter set fairly in they met no more, for the elder Evelina was taken ill, and her young cousin did not leave her even to go to meeting. People said they guessed it was Evelina Adams's last sickness, and they furthermore guessed that she would divide her property between her cousin Martha Loomis and her two girls and Evelina Leonard, and that Evelina would have the house as her share.

Thomas Merriam heard this last
with a satisfaction which he did not
try to disguise from himself, because
he never dreamed of there being any
selfish element in it.   It was all for
Evelina.   Many a time he had
looked about the humble house
where he had been born, and where
he would have to take Evelina after
he had married her, and striven to
see its poor features with her eyes—
not with his, for which familiarity
had tempered them.   Often, as he
sat with his parents in the old sitting-room, in which he had kept so
far an unquestioning belief, as in a
friend of his childhood, the scales of
his own personality would fall suddenly from his eyes.   Then he would
see, as Evelina, the poor, worn,
humble face of his home, and his
heart would sink.   " I don't see
how I ever can bring her here," he
thought.   He began to save, a few
cents at a time, out of his pitiful

salary, to at least beautify his own
chamber a little when Evelina should
come. He made up his mind that
she should have a little dressing-
table, with an oval mirror, and a
white muslin frill around it, like one
he had seen in Boston. " She shall
have that to sit before while she
combs her hair," he thought, with
defiant tenderness, when he stowed
away another shilling in a little box
in his trunk. It was money which
he ordinarily bestowed upon foreign
missions; but his Evelina had come
between him and the heathen. To
procure some dainty furnishings for
her bridal-chamber he took away a
good half of his tithes for the spread
of the gospel in the dark lands.
Now and then his conscience smote
him, he felt shamefaced before his
deacons, but Evelina kept her first
claim. He resolved that another
year he would hire a piece of land,
and combine farming with his

ministerial work, and so try to eke
out his salary, and get a little
more money to beautify his poor
home for his bride.

Now if Evelina Adams had come
to the appointed time for the closing
of her solitary life, and if her young
cousin should inherit a share of her
goodly property and the fine old
mansion-house, all necessity for
anxiety of this kind was over.
Young Evelina would not need to
be taken away, for the sake of her
love, from all these comforts and
luxuries. Thomas Merriam rejoiced
innocently, without a thought for
himself.

In the course of the winter he
confided in his father; he could n't
keep it to himself any longer. Then
there was another reason. Seeing
Evelina so little made him at times
almost doubt the reality of it all.
There were days when he was de-
pressed, and inclined to ask himself

if he had not dreamed it. Telling somebody gave it substance.

His father listened soberly when he told him; he had grown old of late.

" Well," said he, " she 'ain't been used to living the way you have, though you have had advantages that none of your folks ever had; but if she likes you, that 's all there is to it, I s'pose."

The old man sighed wearily. He sat in his arm-chair at the kitchen fireplace; his wife had gone in to one of the neighbors, and the two were alone.

" Of course," said Thomas, simply, " if Evelina Adams should n't live, the chances are that I should n't have to bring her here. She would n't have to give up anything on my account—you know that, father."

Then the young man started, for his father turned suddenly on him with a pale, wrathful face. " You

ain't countin' on that!'' he shouted.
"You ain't countin' on that—a son
of mine countin' on anything like
that!''

Thomas colored. "Why, father,"
he stammered, "you don't think—
you know, it 's all for *her*—and they
say she can't live anyway. I had
never thought of such a thing before. I was wondering how I could
make it comfortable for Evelina
here.''

But his father did not seem to
listen. "Countin' on that!'' he repeated. "Countin' on a poor old
soul, that 'ain't ever had anything
to set her heart on but a few posies,
dyin' to make room for other folks
to have what she 's been cheated
out on. Countin' on that!'' The
old man's voice broke into a hoarse
sob; he got up, and went hurriedly
out of the room.

"Why, father!'' his son called
after him, in alarm. He got up to

follow him, but his father waved him back and shut the door hard.

" Father must be getting child-ish," Thomas thought, wonder-ingly. He did not bring up the subject to him again.

Evelina Adams died in March. One morning the bell tolled seventy long melancholy tones before people had eaten their breakfasts. They ran to their doors and counted. " It 's her," they said, nodding, when they had waited a little after the seventieth stroke. Directly Mrs. Martha Loomis and her two girls were seen hustling importantly down the road, with their shawls over their heads, to the Squire's house. " Mis' Loomis can lay her out," they said. " It ain't likely that young Evelina knows anything about such things. Guess she 'll be thankful she 's got somebody to call on now, if she 'ain't mixed much with the Loomises." Then they wondered when the

funeral would be, and the women
furbished up their black gowns and
bonnets, and even in a few cases
drove to the next town and borrowed
from relatives; but there was a great
disappointment in store for them.

Evelina Adams died on a Satur-
day. The next day it was announced
from the pulpit that the funeral
would be private, by the particular
request of the deceased. Evelina
Adams had carried her delicate
seclusion beyond death, to the very
borders of the grave. Nobody, outside the family, was bidden to the
funeral, except the doctor, the minister, and the two deacons of the
church. They were to be the bearers.
The burial also was to be private, in
the Squire's family burial-lot, at the
north of the house. The bearers
would carry the coffin across the
yard, and there would not only be
no funeral, but no funeral proces-
sion, and no hearse. " It don't

seem scarcely decent," the women whispered to each other; " and more than all that, she ain't goin' to be *seen*." The deacons' wives were especially disturbed by this last, as they might otherwise have gained many interesting particulars by proxy.

Monday was the day set for the burial. Early in the morning old Thomas Merriam walked feebly up the road to the Squire's house. People noticed him as he passed. " How terribly fast he 's grown old lately!" they said. He opened the gate which led into the Squire's front yard with fumbling fingers, and went up the walk to the front door, under the Corinthian pillars, and raised the brass knocker.

Evelina opened the door, and started and blushed when she saw him. She had been crying; there were red rings around her blue eyes, and her pretty lips were swollen.

She tried to smile at Thomas's father, and she held out her hand with shy welcome.

" I want to see her," the old man said, abruptly.

Evelina started, and looked at him wonderingly. " I—don't believe— I know who you mean," said she. "Do you want to see Mrs. Loomis?"

" No; I want to see her."

" *Her?* "

" Yes, *her.*"

Evelina turned pale as she stared at him. There was something strange about his face. " But—Cousin Evelina," she faltered—" she—did n't want— Perhaps you don't know: she left special directions that nobody was to look at her."

" I *want to see her*," said the old man, and Evelina gave way. She stood aside for him to enter, and led him into the great north parlor, where Evelina Adams lay in her mournful state. The shutters were

closed, and one on entering could
distinguish nothing but that long
black shadow in the middle of the
room. Young Evelina opened a
shutter a little way, and a slanting
shaft of spring sunlight came in and
shot athwart the coffin. The old
man tiptoed up and leaned over
and looked at the dead woman.
Evelina Adams had left further in-
structions about her funeral, which
no one understood, but which were
faithfully carried out. She wished,
she had said, to be attired for her
long sleep in a certain rose-colored
gown, laid away in rose leaves and
lavender in a certain chest in a certain chamber. There were also
silken hose and satin shoes with it,
and these were to be put on, and a
wrought lace tucker fastened with a
pearl brooch.

It was the costume she had worn
one Sabbath day back in her youth,
when she had looked across the

meeting-house and her eyes had met young Thomas Merriam's; but nobody knew nor remembered; even young Evelina thought it was simply a vagary of her dead cousin's.

" It don't seem to me decent to lay away anybody dressed so," said Mrs. Martha Loomis ; " but of course last wishes must be respected."

The two Loomis girls said they were thankful nobody was to see the departed in her rose-colored shroud.

Even old Thomas Merriam, leaning over poor Evelina, cold and dead in the garb of her youth, did not remember it, and saw no meaning in it.   He looked at her long. The beautiful color was all faded out of the yellow-white face; the sweet full lips were set and thin; the closed blue eyes sunken in dark hollows; the yellow hair showed a line of gray at the edge of her old woman's cap, and thin gray curls

lay against the hollow cheeks. But
old Thomas Merriam drew a long
breath when he looked at her. It
was like a gasp of admiration and
wonder; a strange rapture came into
his dim eyes; his lips moved as if he
whispered to her, but young Evelina could not hear a sound. She
watched him, half frightened, but
finally he turned to her. "I 'ain't
seen her—fairly," said he, hoarsely
—"I 'ain't seen her, savin' a glimpse
of her at the window, for over forty
year, and she 'ain't changed, not a
look. I 'd have known her anywheres. She 's the same as she was
when she was a girl. It 's wonderful
—wonderful!"

Young Evelina shrank a little.
"We think she looks natural," she
said, hesitatingly.

"She looks jest as she did when
she was a girl and used to come into
the meetin'-house. She *is* jest the
same," the old man repeated, in his

eager, hoarse voice. Then he bent over the coffin, and his lips moved again. Young Evelina would have called Mrs. Loomis, for she was frightened, had he not been Thomas's father, and had it not been for her vague feeling that there might be some old story to explain this which she had never heard. " Maybe he was in love with poor Cousin Evelina, as Thomas is with me," thought young Evelina, using her own leaping-pole of love to land straight at the truth. But she never told her surmise to any one except Thomas, and that was long afterwards, when the old man was dead. Now she watched him with her blue dilated eyes. But soon he turned away from the coffin and made his way straight out of the room, without a word. Evelina followed him through the entry and opened the outer door. He turned on the threshold and looked back at her, his face working.

" Don't ye go to lottin' too much on what ye 're goin' to get through folks that have died an' not had anything," he said; and he shook his head almost fiercely at her.

" No, I won't. I don't think I understand what you mean, sir," stammered Evelina.

The old man stood looking at her a moment. Suddenly she saw the tears rolling over his old cheeks. " I 'm much obliged to ye for lettin' of me see her," he said, hoarsely, and crept feebly down the steps.

Evelina went back trembling to the room where her dead cousin lay, and covered her face, and closed the shutter again. Then she went about her household duties, wondering. She could not understand what it all meant; but one thing she understood—that in some way this old dead woman, Evelina Adams, had gotten immortal youth and beauty in one human heart. " She looked to him just as she did when she was a girl," Evelina kept thinking to herself with awe. She said nothing about it to Mrs. Martha Loomis or her daughters. They had been in the back part of the house, and had not heard old Thomas Merriam come in, and they never knew about it.

Mrs. Loomis and the two girls stayed in the house day and night until after the funeral. They confidently expected to live there in the future. "It is n't likely that Evelina Adams thought a young woman no older than Evelina Leonard could live here alone in this great house with nobody but that old Sarah Judd. It would not be proper nor becoming," said Martha Loomis to her two daughters; and they agreed, and brought over many of their possessions under cover of night to the Squire's house during the interval before the funeral.

But after the funeral and the reading of the will the Loomises made sundry trips after dusk back to their old home, with their best petticoats and cloaks over their arms, and their bonnets dangling by their strings at their sides. For Evelina Adams's last will and testament had been read, and therein provision was made for the continuance of the annuity heretofore paid them for their support, with the condition affixed that not one night should they spend after the reading of the will in the house known as the Squire Adams house. The annuity was an ample one, and would provide the widow Martha Loomis and her daughters, as it had done before, with all the needfuls of life; but upon hearing the will they stiffened their double chins into their kerchiefs with indignation, for they had looked for more.

Evelina Adams's will was a will of

conditions, for unto it she had affixed two more, and those affected her beloved cousin Evelina Leonard. It was notable that " beloved " had not preceded her cousin Martha Loomis's name in the will. No pretence of love, when she felt none, had she ever made in her life. The entire property of Evelina Adams, spinster, deceased, with the exception of Widow Martha Loomis's provision, fell to this beloved young Evelina Leonard, subject to two conditions—firstly, she was never to enter into matrimony, with any person whomsoever, at any time whatsoever; secondly, she was never to let the said spinster Evelina Adams's garden, situated at the rear and southward of the house known as the Squire Adams house, die through any neglect of hers. Due allowance was to be made for the dispensations of Providence: for hail and withering frost and long-

94

continued drought, and for times wherein the said Evelina Leonard might, by reason of being confined to the house by sickness, be prevented from attending to the needs of the growing plants, and the verdict in such cases was to rest with the minister and the deacons of the church. But should this beloved Evelina love and wed, or should she let, through any wilful neglect, that garden perish in the season of flowers, all that goodly property would she forfeit to a person unknown, whose name, enclosed in a sealed envelope, was to be held meantime in the hands of the executor, who had also drawn up the will, Lawyer Joshua Lang.

There was great excitement in the village over this strange and unwonted will. Some were there who held that Evelina Adams had not been of sound mind, and it should be contested. It was even rumored that

Widow Martha Loomis had visited
Lawyer Joshua Lang and broached
the subject, but he had dismissed
the matter peremptorily by telling
her that Evelina Adams, spinster, deceased, had been as much in her right
mind at the time of drawing the will
as anybody of his acquaintance.

" Not setting store by relations,
and not wanting to have them under
your roof, does n't go far in law nor
common-sense to send folks to the
madhouse," old Lawyer Lang, who
was famed for his sharp tongue, was
reported to have said. However,
Mrs. Martha Loomis was somewhat
comforted by her firm belief that
either her own name or that of one
of her daughters was in that sealed
envelope kept by Lawyer Joshua
Lang in his strong-box, and by her
firm purpose to watch carefully lest
Evelina prove derelict in fulfilling
the two conditions whereby she held
the property.

Larger peep-holes were soon cut away mysteriously in the high arborvitæ hedge, and therein were often set for a few moments, when they passed that way, the eager eyes of Mrs. Martha or her daughter Flora or Fidelia Loomis. Frequent calls they also made upon Evelina, living alone with the old woman Sarah Judd, who had been called in during her cousin's illness, and they strolled into the garden, spying anxiously for withered leaves or dry stalks. They at every opportunity interviewed the old man who assisted Evelina in her care of the garden concerning its welfare. But small progress they made with him, standing digging at the earth with his spade while they talked, as if in truth his wits had gone therein before his body and he would uncover them.

Moreover, Mrs. Martha Loomis talked much slyly to mothers of

young men, and sometimes with
bold insinuations to the young men
themselves, of the sad lot of poor
young Evelina, condemned to a
solitary and loveless life, and of her
sweetness and beauty and desirabil-
ity in herself, although she could not
bring the old Squire's money to her
husband. And once, but no more
than that, she touched lightly upon
the subject to the young minister,
Thomas Merriam, when he was
making a pastoral call.

" My heart bleeds for the poor
child living all alone in that great
house," said she. And she looked
down mournfully, and did not see
how white the young minister's face
turned. " It seems almost a pity,"
said she, furthermore—" Evelina is
a good housekeeper, and has rare
qualities in herself, and so many get
poor wives nowadays — that some
godly young man should not court
her in spite of the will. I doubt,

too, if she would not have a happier
lot than growing old over that garden, as poor Cousin Evelina did before her, even if she has a fine house
to live in and a goodly sum in the
bank. She looks pindling enough
lately. I 'll warrant she has lost a
good ten pound since poor Evelina
was laid away, and—''

But Thomas Merriam cut her
short. '' I see no profit in discuss-
ing matters which do not concern
us,'' said he, and only his ministerial
estate saved him from the charge of
impertinence.

As it was, Martha Loomis colored
high. '' I 'll warrant he' ll look out
which side his bread is buttered on;
ministers always do,'' she said to her
daughters after he had gone. She
never dreamed how her talk had cut
him to the heart.

Had he not seen more plainly than
any one else, Sunday after Sunday,
when he glanced down at her once

or twice cautiously from his pulpit,
how weary-looking and thin she was
growing ?   And her bright color was
wellnigh gone, and there were pitiful
downward lines at the corners of her
sweet mouth.   Poor young Evelina
was fading like one of her own
flowers, as if some celestial gardener
had failed in his care of her.   And
Thomas saw it, and in his heart of
hearts he knew the reason, and yet
he would not yield.   Not once had
he entered the old Squire's house
since he attended the dead Evelina's
funeral, and stood praying and
eulogizing, with her coffin between
him and the living Evelina, with her
pale face shrouded in black bombazine.   He had never spoken to her
since, nor entered the house; but
he had written her a letter, in which
all the fierce passion and anguish of
his heart was cramped and held
down by formal words and phrases,
and poor young Evelina did not see

beneath them. When her lover wrote her that he felt it inconsistent with his Christian duty and the higher aims of his existence to take any further steps towards a matrimonial alliance, she felt merely that Thomas either cared no more for her, or had come to consider, upon due reflection, that she was not fit to undertake the responsible position of a minister's wife. " It may be that in some way I failed in my attendance upon Cousin Evelina," thought poor young Evelina, " or it may be that he thinks I have not enough dignity of character to inspire respect among the older women in the church." And sometimes, with a sharp thrust of misery that shook her out of her enforced patience and meekness, she wondered if indeed her own loving freedom with him had turned him against her, and led him in his later and sober judgment to consider her too light-minded for a minister's wife. " It may be that I was guilty of great indecorum, and almost indeed forfeited my claim to respect for maidenly modesty, inasmuch as I suffered him to give me kisses, and did almost bring myself to return them in kind. But my heart did so entreat me, and in truth it seemed almost like a lack of sincerity for me to wholly withstand it," wrote poor young Evelina in her journal at that time; and she further wrote: " It is indeed hard for one who has so little knowledge to be fully certain of what is or is not becoming and a Christian duty in matters of this kind; but if I have in any manner, through my ignorance or unwarrantable affection, failed, and so lost the love and respect of a good man, and the opportunity to become his help-meet during life, I pray that I may be forgiven—for I sinned not wilfully —that the lesson may be sanctified unto me, and that I may live as the Lord order, in Christian patience and meekness, and not repining." It never occurred to young Evelina that possibly Thomas Merriam's sense of duty might be strengthened by the loss of all her cousin's property should she marry him, and neither did she dream that he might hesitate to take her from affluence into poverty for her own sake. For herself the property, as put in the balance beside her love, was lighter than air itself. It was so light that it had no place in her consciousness. She simply had thought, upon hearing the will, of Martha Loomis and her daughters in possession of the property, and herself with Thomas, with perfect acquiescence and rapture.

Evelina Adams's disapprobation of her marriage, which was supposedly expressed in the will, had indeed, without reference to the

property, somewhat troubled her
tender heart, but she told herself
that Cousin Evelina had not known
she had promised to marry Thomas;
that she would not wish her to break
her solemn promise. And furthermore, it seemed to her quite reason-
able that the condition had been
inserted in the will mainly through
concern for the beloved garden.

" Cousin Evelina might have
thought perhaps I would let the
flowers die when I had a husband
and children to take care of," said
Evelina. And so she had disposed
of all the considerations which had
disturbed her, and had thought of
no others.

She did not answer Thomas's
letter. It was so worded that it
seemed to require no reply, and she
felt that he must be sure of her acquiescence in whatever he thought
best. She laid the letter away in a
little rosewood box, in which she

had always kept her dearest treasures since her school-days. Sometimes she took it out and read it, and it seemed to her that the pain in her heart would put an end to her in spite of all her prayers for Christian fortitude; and yet she could not help reading it again.

It was seldom that she stole a look at her old lover as he stood in the pulpit in the meeting-house, but when she did she thought with an anxious pang that he looked worn and ill, and that night she prayed that the Lord would restore his health to him for the sake of his people.

It was four months after Evelina Adams's death, and her garden was in the full glory of midsummer, when one evening, towards dusk, young Evelina went slowly down the street. She seldom walked abroad now, but kept herself almost as secluded as her cousin had done before her. But that night a great restlessness was

upon her, and she put a little black
silk shawl over her shoulders and
went out. It was quite cool, although it was midsummer. The
dusk was deepening fast; the katydids called back and forth from the
wayside bushes. Evelina met nobody for some distance. Then she
saw a man coming towards her, and
her heart stood still, and she was
about to turn back, for she thought
for a minute it was the young minister. Then she saw it was his father,
and she went on slowly, with her
eyes downcast. When she met him
she looked up and said good-evening, gravely, and would have passed
on, but he stood in her way.

" I 've got a word to say to ye, if
ye 'll listen," he said.

Evelina looked at him tremblingly.
There was something strained and
solemn in his manner. " I 'll hear
whatever you have to say, sir," she
said.

The old man leaned his pale face over her and raised a shaking fore-finger. " I 've made up my mind to say something," said he. " I don't know as I 've got any right to, and maybe my son will blame me, but I 'm goin' to see that you have a chance. It 's been borne in upon me that women folks don't always have a fair chance. It 's jest this I 'm goin' to say: I don't know whether you know how my son feels about it or not. I don't know how open he 's been with you. Do you know jest why he quit you ?"

Evelina shook her head. " No," she panted — " I don't — I never knew. He said it was his duty."

" Duty can get to be an idol of wood and stone, an' I don't know but Thomas's is," said the old man. " Well, I 'll tell you. He don't think it 's right for him to marry you, and make you leave that big house, and lose all that money. He don't care anything about it for himself, but it 's for you. Did you know that ?''

Evelina grasped the old man's arm hard with her little fingers.

'' You don't mean that—was why he did it!'' she gasped.

'' Yes, that was why.''

Evelina drew away from him. She was ashamed to have Thomas's father see the joy in her face. '' Thank you, sir,'' she said. '' I did not understand. I—will write to him.''

'' Maybe my son will think I have done wrong coming betwixt him and his idees of duty,'' said old Thomas Merriam, '' but sometimes there 's a good deal lost for lack of a word, and I wanted you to have a fair chance an' a fair say. It 's been borne in upon me that women folks don't always have it. Now you can do jest as you think best, but you must remember one thing—riches ain't all. A little likin' for you that 's

goin' to last, and keep honest and
faithful to you as long as you live, is
worth more; an' it 's worth more to
women folks than 't is to men, an'
it 's worth enough to them. My
son 's poorly. His mother and I are
worried about him. He don't eat
nor sleep—walks his chamber nights.
His mother don't know what the
matter is, but he let on to me some
time since."

"I 'll write a letter to him,"
gasped Evelina again. "Good-
night, sir." She pulled her little
black silk shawl over her head and
hastened home, and all night long
her candle burned, while her weary
little fingers toiled over pages of
foolscap-paper to convince Thomas
Merriam fully, and yet in terms not
exceeding maidenly reserve, that the
love of his heart and the companion-
ship of his life were worth more to
her than all the silver and gold in
the world. Then the next morning

she despatched it, all neatly folded
and sealed, and waited.

It was strange that a letter like
that could not have moved Thomas
Merriam, when his heart too pleaded
with him so hard to be moved. But
that might have been the very reason
why he could withstand her, and why
the consciousness of his own weakness gave him strength. Thomas
Merriam was one, when he had once
fairly laid hold of duty, to grasp it
hard, although it might be to his
own pain and death, and maybe to
that of others. He wrote to poor
young Evelina another letter, in
which he emphasized and repeated
his strict adherence to what he be-
lieved the line of duty in their
separation, and ended it with a
prayer for her welfare and happi-
ness, in which, indeed, for a second,
the passionate heart of the man
showed forth. Then he locked himself in his chamber, and nobody ever

knew what he suffered there. But one pang he did not suffer which Evelina would have suffered in his place. He mourned not over nor realized the grief of her tender heart when she should read his letter, otherwise he could not have sent it. He writhed under his own pain alone, and his duty hugged him hard, like the iron maiden of the old tortures, but he would not yield.

As for Evelina, when she got his letter, and had read it through, she sat still and white for a long time, and did not seem to hear when old Sarah Judd spoke to her. But at last she rose and went to her chamber, and knelt down, and prayed for a long time; and then she went out in the garden and cut all the most beautiful flowers, and tied them in wreaths and bouquets, and carried them out to the north side of the house, where her cousin Evelina was buried, and covered her grave with them. And then she knelt down there, and hid her face among them, and said, in a low voice, as if in a listening ear, " I pray you, Cousin Evelina, forgive me for what I am about to do."

And then she returned to the house, and sat at her needlework as usual; but the old woman kept looking at her, and asking if she were sick, for there was a strange look in her face.

She and old Sarah Judd had always their tea at five o'clock, and put the candles out at nine, and this night they did as they were wont. But at one o'clock in the morning young Evelina stole softly down the stairs with her lighted candle, and passed through into the kitchen; and a half-hour after she came forth into the garden, which lay in full moonlight, and she had in her hand a steaming teakettle, and she passed around among the shrubs and watered them, and a white cloud of steam rose around them. Back and forth she went to the kitchen; for she had heated the great copper wash-kettle full of water; and she watered all the shrubs in the garden, moving amid curling white wreaths of steam, until the water was gone. And then she set to work and tore up by the roots with her little hands and trampled with her little feet all the beautiful tender flower-beds; all the time weeping, and moaning softly: " Poor Cousin Evelina! poor Cousin Evelina! Oh, forgive me, poor Cousin Evelina! "

And at dawn the garden lay in ruin, for all the tender plants she had torn up by the roots and trampled down, and all the stronger-rooted shrubs she had striven to kill with boiling water and salt.

Then Evelina went into the house, and made herself tidy as well as she could when she trembled so,

H

and put her little shawl over her
head, and went down the road to the
Merriams' house. It was so early
the village was scarcely astir, but
there was smoke coming out of the
kitchen chimney at the Merriams';
and when she knocked, Mrs. Merriam opened the door at once, and
stared at her.

" Is Sarah Judd dead ? " she
cried; for her first thought was that
something must have happened
when she saw the girl standing
there with her wild pale face.

" I want to see the minister," said
Evelina, faintly, and she looked at
Thomas's mother with piteous eyes.

" Be you sick ? " asked Mrs. Merriam. She laid a hard hand on the
girl's arm, and led her into the sitting-room, and put her into the
rocking-chair with the feather cush-
ion. " You look real poorly," said
she. " Sha'n't I get you a little of
my elderberry wine ? "

" I want to see him," said Evelina, and she almost sobbed.

" I 'll go right and speak to him,"
said Mrs. Merriam. " He 's up, I
guess. He gets up early to write.
But had n't I better get you something to take first ? You do look
sick."

But Evelina only shook her head.
She had her face covered with her
hands, and was weeping softly.
Mrs. Merriam left the room, with a
long backward glance at her. Presently the door opened and Thomas
came in. Evelina stood up before
him. Her pale face was all wet
with tears, but there was an air of
strange triumph about her.

" The garden is dead," said she.

" What do you mean ? " he cried
out, staring at her, for indeed he
thought for a minute that her wits
had left her.

' The garden is dead," said she.
" Last night I watered the roses

with boiling water and salt, and I pulled the other flowers up by their roots. The garden is dead, and I have lost all Cousin Evelina's money, and it need not come between us any longer." She said that, and looked up in his face with her blue eyes, through which the love of the whole race of loving women from which she had sprung, as well as her own, seemed to look, and held out her little hands; but even then Thomas Merriam could not understand, and stood looking at her.

"Why — did you do it?" he stammered.

"Because you would have me no other way, and—I could n't bear that anything like that should come between us," she said, and her voice shook like a harp-string, and her pale face went red, then pale again.

But Thomas still stood staring at her. Then her heart failed her. She thought that he did not care, and she had been mistaken. She felt as if it were the hour of her death, and turned to go. And then he caught her in his arms.

" Oh," he cried, with a great sob, " the Lord make me worthy of thee, Evelina! "

There had never been so much excitement in the village as when the fact of the ruined garden came to light. Flora Loomis, peeping through the hedge on her way to the store, had spied it first. Then she had run home for her mother, who had in turn sought Lawyer Lang, panting bonnetless down the road. But before the lawyer had started for the scene of disaster, the minister, Thomas Merriam, had appeared, and asked for a word in private with him. Nobody ever knew just what that word was, but the lawyer was singularly uncommunicative and reticent as to the ruined garden.

" Do you think the young woman is out of her mind ? " one of the deacons asked him, in a whisper.

" I wish all the young women were as much in their minds; we 'd have a better world," said the lawyer, gruffly.

" When do you think we can begin to move in here ? " asked Mrs. Martha Loomis, her wide skirts sweeping a bed of uprooted verbenas.

" When your claim is established," returned the lawyer, shortly, and turned on his heel and went away, his dry old face scanning the ground like a dog on a scent. That afternoon he opened the sealed document in the presence of witnesses, and the name of the heir to whom the property fell was disclosed. It was " Thomas Merriam, the beloved and esteemed minister of this parish," and young Evelina would gain her wealth instead of losing it by her marriage. And furthermore, after the declaration of the name of the heir was this added: " This do I in the hope and belief that neither the greed of riches nor the fear of them shall prevent that which is good and wise in the sight of the Lord, and with the surety that a love which shall triumph over so much in its way shall endure, and shall be a blessing and not a curse to my beloved cousin, Evelina Leonard."

Thomas Merriam and Evelina were married before the leaves fell in that same year, by the minister of the next village, who rode over in his chaise, and brought his wife, who was also a bride, and wore her wedding-dress of a pink and pearl shot silk. But young Evelina wore the blue bridal array which had been worn by old Squire Adams's bride, all remodelled daintily to suit the fashion of the times; and as she moved, the fragrances of roses and lavender of the old summers during which it had been laid away were evident, like sweet memories.

THE END

LITTLE BOOKS
BY FAMOUS WRITERS

Uniform with this Volume—with Frontispiece
Fifty Cents a Volume

HARPER & BROTHERS, PUBLISHERS
NEW YORK AND LONDON

☞ *Any of the above works will be sent by mail,
postage prepaid, to any part of the United States, Canada, or Mexico, on receipt of the price.*